THE *DIARY OF A WIMPY KID* SERIES

MORE FROM THE *WIMPY* WORLD

DIARY of a Wimpy Kid

BIG SHOT

by Jeff Kinney

AMULET BOOKS

New York

Cataloging-in-Publication Data has been applied for and may be obtained from the Library of Congress.

ISBN 978-1-4197-4915-5

Veggie Rocker characters on page 46 created by Daryl Enos. Used with permission and gratitude.

Book design by Jeff Kinney
Cover design by Jeff Kinney and Brenda E. Angelilli

Printed and bound in U.S.A.
10 9 8 7 6 5 4 3 2 1

Amulet Books are available at special discounts when purchased in quantity for premiums and promotions as well as fundraising or educational use. Special editions can also be created to specification. For details, contact specialsales@abramsbooks.com or the address below.

ABRAMS The Art of Books
195 Broadway, New York, NY 10007
abramsbooks.com

TO WILL AND GRANT

SEPTEMBER

<u>Monday</u>

I've heard that athletes are born with special genes that make them good at sports. Well, whatever those genes are, I guess I was born WITHOUT them.

Mom's always saying that everyone who's part of a team has an important role to play. But when it comes to sports, it seems like my job is to make everybody ELSE look good.

At this point in my life, I'm pretty sure I'm not gonna grow up to become a professional athlete. So I'm officially announcing my retirement.

The crazy thing is, I used to actually LIKE sports. But that was back in preschool, when sports were still FUN. The first sport I ever played was soccer. I didn't know the rules, but neither did any of the other kids. So most of the time it was just pure chaos on the field.

BOOP

Wherever the ball went, we all chased after it. Every once in a while the ball would pop out of the pack and go in someone's goal, then EVERYONE would celebrate.

FLING

BLUB BLUB

Nobody kept score, so you never knew who was winning or losing. And the parents didn't care because they were too busy doing their own thing.

The referees were middle-school kids, and they didn't really pay attention to the game, either.

In fact, the refs didn't even blow their whistles when the ball went out of bounds. So half the time we'd be playing on the wrong field and didn't KNOW it.

After the game, we'd always get slushies and junk food at the snack shack. And sometimes we wouldn't even wait for the game to be OVER to treat ourselves.

The coaches were really nice and made sure everyone got a chance to score. And that made everyone feel good about themselves.

Back then, I was SURE I was gonna grow up to be a professional soccer player. I even kept my rookie card in mint condition in case it turned out to be worth something one day.

But when we got to kindergarten, everything CHANGED. The refs started using their whistles, and they didn't let us do the kinds of things we got away with the year before.

That season, the refs blew their whistles almost every time I touched the ball. So when I was in the game, I'd stand in the corner of the field and pray the ball didn't roll to me.

It's not like I was getting a lot of playing time in kindergarten anyway. The coach only put in the kids who were GOOD, and the rest of us sat on the bench.

Mom told me the reason the coach wasn't playing me was because I was his "secret weapon" and he was saving me for a big moment.

But I didn't understand that Mom was just trying to make me feel better about myself. So whenever the coach DID put me in the game, I'd go out there thinking I was hot stuff.

Even the snack shack wasn't fun that year. Some parents complained that they were selling too much junk food, so they replaced the slushies and other sugary treats with HEALTHY options.

But the slushie sales from the snack shack paid for the field upkeep. So that year the parks department could only afford to mow the grass once every three weeks, which really slowed the games down.

After a bunch of kids got ticks from playing soccer in the long grass, they decided to end the season early, which was totally fine with ME.

I feel bad that I've never been good at sports, because I think Dad was hoping I'd be a star athlete. Whenever he'd go to the library, he'd always come home with a stack of sports books.

I'm sure there are kids who are into those types of stories, but that was never ME.

If you go to the library, you'll find all sorts of books about kids who do amazing things and lead their teams to victory. But I never had any experiences like that, and I'll bet there are lots of kids out there just like me.

So one of these days somebody should write a book for the REST of us.

It's not like I've got anything against sports. I like them just fine, as long as I'm not the one PLAYING. In fact, this summer I watched the Olympics on TV pretty much nonstop.

It was Mom's idea for us to watch the games as a family. She says that these days everyone's in their own little bubbles, and sports is one of the only things that can still bring people together. But I think a little togetherness goes a long way.

Mom says she loves the Olympics because they show what human beings are capable of at their best. But I like watching for the BLOOPERS.

I'm just glad it's somebody ELSE out there and not ME. Because I'm sure I'd be nervous if I knew there were millions of people watching from home. And when you mess up in the Olympics, you're supposed to act graceful about it.

But if I just spent four years of my life training and then made some dumb mistake, I'm pretty sure I'd have trouble smiling for the cameras.

That's why I'd do one of those sports where you're part of a TEAM. Because then, when you screw up, it's harder for people to tell.

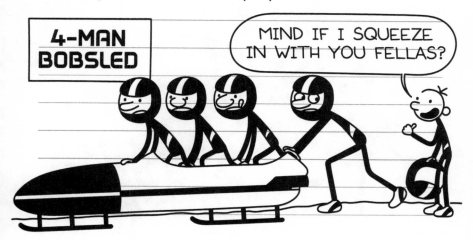

In fact, if I was in the Olympics, I'd be in one of those events where a HORSE is involved. Because then if something goes wrong, at least you'd have someone to BLAME.

But now that I think about it, that's probably the reason why horses sometimes act out.

Even though we watched a lot of Olympics coverage,
I still don't understand the way everything works.

For one thing, I don't see why they only hand
out medals to the athletes who take the top three
spots in a competition. It seems to me like they
could keep going with the medals so EVERYONE
goes home with a prize.

15th PLACE: ALUMINUM MEDAL

GREG
HEFFLEY

The way it is right now, they give you a gold
medal if you take first place, silver if you take
second, and bronze if you take third. But I feel
like there's a pretty big step down between silver
and bronze.

At least gold and silver are WORTH something. But if you won a bronze medal, you'd be lucky to get a few bucks for it.

I figure the moment your medal is the most valuable is right after you WIN it. So if I got one, I'd try to take advantage of the TV audience and find a buyer.

During the medal ceremony they have the top three athletes stand on a podium, and then they play the gold medalist's national anthem and make the other two athletes stand there and listen. But if I took silver or bronze, I'd pop in some earbuds so I could jam to my own tunes.

One of Mom's favorite things about the Olympics is when they tell the life stories of the athletes who are competing. Some of the stories are really inspiring, because a lot of these athletes had to overcome tough challenges to get where they are.

But if I ever made it to the Olympics, my story wouldn't be all that inspirational.

GREG HEFFLEY: PARENTS MADE HIM PLAY SPORTS

Mom keeps telling me that one day I could be an Olympian, and I should start my "Olympic journey" now. But I'm pretty sure it's already too LATE for me.

For most sports, you have to start playing really young if you wanna be any good. So even if I got serious, I'm sure I'd be competing with kids who are half my age.

I've heard that in some countries they identify kids with potential SUPER early, and then they send them off to these elite academies to train around the clock.

BOUNCE

I really don't think there's any hope for me of becoming an Olympian. But my brother Manny is only in preschool, so maybe he's still got a shot.

I'm not an expert on this stuff or anything, but from what I've seen, the kid looks like he's got POTENTIAL.

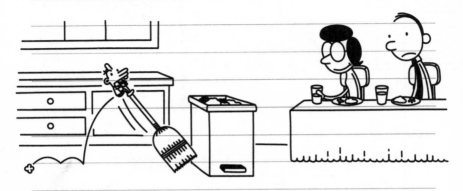

To be honest, I wouldn't mind if Mom and Dad shipped Manny off to one of those sports academies. Because that would be one less person I'd have to share a bathroom with.

VROOM
ACADEMY

But maybe there are some sports that you can start when you're a little older, and there's still hope for a person like me. Because it would be pretty cool to represent your country as an Olympian, no matter WHAT sport you compete in.

And if I won a GOLD medal, you can bet I'd never take it OFF.

When you win a gold medal, you're set for LIFE. And even when your Olympic career is over, you can still make a fortune doing appearances and signing stuff.

But the real money's in advertising products on TV. And I'd say yes to EVERYTHING as long as the money was good.

The best thing about being an athlete is that you can retire YOUNG. And that would be great for a person like me, because there are lots of places I'd like to visit and things I'd like to see.

So I'm not going to give up on sports just yet. Because who knows? Maybe I could be a person everyone looks up to.

Tuesday

It turns out I'm gonna have a chance to prove myself sooner than I THOUGHT. When we got back to school after summer vacation, there were posters in the hallways announcing Field Day.

CALLING ALL ATHLETES!

GO

TEAM

FIELD DAY

IS ALMOST HERE!

NEXT WEDNESDAY @ 1:30 P.M.

They have Field Day at my middle school every four years, and the last time they held it was when my brother Rodrick was my age. I remember him getting excited about the competition because the winning homeroom got free ice cream at lunch.

Well, this year they've raised the stakes. If your homeroom wins the competition, your class gets a day off from school. So that has everyone motivated to WIN.

SPROING

BOING BOING

But the person who wants the day off the MOST is Mrs. Bosh, my homeroom teacher. She's pregnant and is always telling us how hard it is to be on her feet all day.

Well, I could use a day off from school, too. I don't want to let Mrs. Bosh or the rest of my team down, so I'm actually taking this competition pretty SERIOUSLY.

The thing is, I'm not in the best shape right now. So unless I do something about it, I won't be able to help us on the big day.

I told Dad I wanted to get in shape, and he said I could start going to the gym with HIM. I'm not trying to be rude or anything, but Dad's been going to the same gym for years, and whatever he's doing there doesn't really look like it's WORKING.

But I figured anything would be better than what I've been doing for exercise, which is nothing. So after dinner I threw on some workout clothes and tagged along with Dad.

The gym was packed, but I noticed there weren't any people MY age there. Dad told me that technically kids aren't allowed at the gym, but if I didn't call attention to myself I should be OK.

GRUNT!

There was all sorts of fancy equipment that I couldn't wait to try out. But Dad said it was best to start off slow, and he took me to the area of the gym where he likes to work out.

When Dad showed me his exercise routine, I could understand why he hasn't been getting any RESULTS.

After Dad did a few sit-ups and jumping jacks, he said he was gonna go relax in the sauna for a while. And that meant I was free to exercise on my own.

But the thing is, I didn't really know how to use any of the machines, because they were all too complicated.

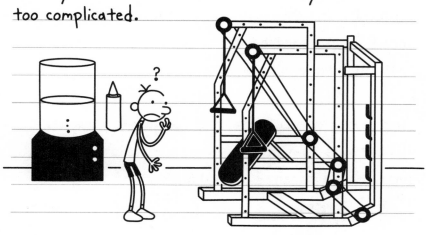

So I had to try and figure things out for MYSELF, and I'm still not a hundred percent sure I was using the equipment the right way.

GRUNT!

What I really wanted to do was try out some of the things with SCREENS on them, like the treadmills and the elliptical machines. But people were hogging that equipment and staying on longer than they were supposed to.

And even when I gave them a gentle reminder that it was time to let someone ELSE have a turn, nobody seemed to take the hint.

While I waited for one of the machines to open up, I passed the time by watching television. But the TVs were all tuned to some boring business show.

So I found the remote and changed the channel to something a little more INTERESTING.

I guess everyone doesn't have the same taste in entertainment as me, because some lady got off the treadmill to change the channel. But as soon as she stepped off the machine, I jumped at my chance.

There was a big screen on the front of the treadmill, and you could choose between all these famous places to take your walk.

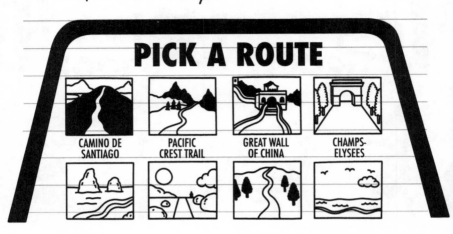

So I spent a few minutes trying to decide where I wanted to GO.

After I made my choice the treadmill started moving, and I felt like I was actually walking along the Great Wall of China.

But I guess the Great Wall is STEEP, and I was having trouble keeping up. So after a while, I put my feet on either side of the conveyor belt and took in the sights the EASY way.

I realized I wasn't making the most of my time at the gym, and I started feeling a little guilty about it. But I didn't know what I should do NEXT, because I was running out of options.

That's when I heard some weird noises coming from the other room, and I went to investigate.

It turns out there was a whole different area of the gym, and it looked like this was where all the SERIOUS people hung out.

I wanted to look like THESE guys, but I didn't know how to get started. And when I went around asking for advice, I found out that nobody was in the mood for chitchat.

After a while, I realized the people in there weren't interested in helping a beginner like me, so I was on my OWN. And the first thing I had to decide was which muscles to start working on.

I figured I should probably focus on my arms and chest, because those are the muscles that make you look like you're in shape.

So I decided I'd start with a few bicep curls and go from there. But I didn't want to overdo it, because at lunch yesterday, Albert Sandy told us about this bodybuilder who blew out a bicep, and I sure didn't want that happening to ME.

It turns out I didn't need to stress about it, because I couldn't even get any of the dumbbells off the rack.

I thought I might have better luck with the bench press, but I couldn't budge the barbell, either. And I have to admit, I was getting a little FRUSTRATED.

By now people were staring at me, and I didn't want to look like I didn't know what I was doing. So I started taking the weights off the barbell to make it a little lighter.

But it turns out you're not supposed to take the weights off one side of the barbell all at ONCE, because when you do, everything slides off the other side. And apparently people in the weight room don't like loud noises.

So I guess that's the reason why they don't let kids in the gym. But it doesn't seem right that they kicked Dad out, too, because he really has been a loyal member.

Thursday

Mom said that when it comes to getting in shape, exercise is only HALF the picture. She said nutrition is just as important, and she'd be happy to teach me a few things about eating right if I really wanted to learn.

I didn't feel like getting a lecture about food, but I jumped at the chance to go with her to the grocery store. And that's because I wanted to help pick out the food we'd have in the pantry.

Whenever Manny goes to the store with Mom, he picks the things HE wants. And that's why we have all this random stuff in our cabinets.

No offense to Mom or anything, but she's TERRIBLE at picking out snacks. She always buys healthy stuff that tastes awful, and she won't buy any NEW snacks until we've eaten all the old ones.

So lately I've been having my best friend, Rowley, over for "tasting parties" to help me clear space in the cabinets.

When we got to the grocery store today, I split off from Mom, then loaded up the cart with a bunch of my favorites. Then I grabbed a few healthy items just to make Mom happy.

But it turns out MY idea of health food isn't the same as MOM'S. When we met back up, she went over each item I picked out and explained why it wasn't good for me.

She held up a bottle of fruit juice, which I thought was a pretty solid choice on my part. But Mom said it was full of SUGAR, and there wasn't any nutritional value to it. I told Mom she was wrong, because there was a picture of tons of different fruits right there on the bottle.

Then Mom showed me the label, and I couldn't believe they can even get away with that.

Mom said that if you really want to know what's in the food you buy, you have to read the list of ingredients. And she told me the cans of Chef Marinara pasta I had in the cart were full of all sorts of CHEMICALS.

But I knew Mom was wrong about THAT one, because I've seen the Chef Marinara ads on television that show him making his pasta by hand in Old Italy.

Mom showed me the small print on the back of the can, which said the food was made in a factory in Detroit. She said Chef Marinara probably wasn't even a real person, and they just hired an actor for those TV ads.

Well, that made me feel pretty stupid for dressing up as Chef Marinara in our Wax Figure Exhibit at school last year.

Then I started to wonder if Rotten Rudy was a real person, because those Rotten Rudy TV ads scared me into drinking a gallon of milk every day.

Mom said food companies are really clever about slipping their advertising into places you wouldn't expect, which made me think about the posters that are up in our hallways at school.

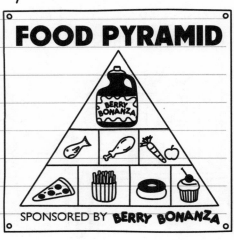

She explained that sometimes packaged food companies use cartoon characters to get young kids to want their products. And I think she's right, because before we left the house today, Manny was watching an episode of "The Murples" where Munchy Murple was chowing down on a bowl of Rock Candy Crunch cereal.

Mom told me that when she buys food for the family, she checks the labels and doesn't buy anything with ingredients she can't pronounce.

Then she said the best thing to do is buy food with only ONE ingredient, like fruits and vegetables.

Well, I don't know if it's just my generation, but it's a little hard for a kid like me to eat something that isn't wrapped in cellophane or doesn't come in a cardboard box. In fact, if chocolate bars grew in the ground, I'll bet I wouldn't TOUCH them.

But if the people who sell fruits and vegetables wanna get kids eating that stuff, they're gonna need to step up their advertising game.

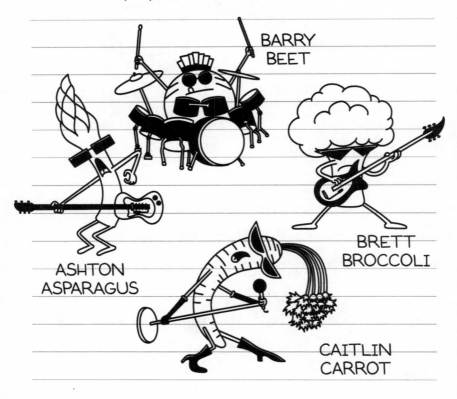

BARRY
BEET

BRETT
BROCCOLI

ASHTON
ASPARAGUS

CAITLIN
CARROT

Tuesday

Field Day is tomorrow, and things have really started to heat up at school.

Mrs. Bosh has been making everyone in our homeroom get to class a half hour early so we have extra time to put together our strategy. And she's been getting paranoid about what the OTHER classrooms are doing to prepare.

So today she sent Ledavian Mills up into the ceiling so he could spy on Mr. Drew's homeroom next door. But it turns out that ceiling tiles aren't strong enough to hold a person's weight.

The homeroom Mrs. Bosh is most worried about is Mrs. Epstein's, because she's got a bunch of athletes in her class. And one of the kids is Jesse Range, who stayed back in eighth grade TWICE just so he could compete in Field Day one more time.

JESSE RANGE

But the team I'm most nervous about is Mr. Ray's class, because that's the morning detention homeroom. And on Field Day, I'm sure those guys are gonna play DIRTY.

To make matters worse, we found out we're going to be competing with GROWN-UPS in this thing. The janitors went to the vice principal and said they wanted to put together their OWN team because they deserve a day off just as much as us students.

I guess that's fair, but the bathrooms have been getting pretty gnarly ever since they started spending all their time TRAINING.

49

And now the lunch ladies are getting in on the act, so the cafeteria has basically turned into a gymnasium.

The homeroom teachers are getting pretty spooked, so they've started TRADING kids to improve their team's chances. Mr. Esper sent the fastest girl in our school, Ava Hollis, to Mrs. Joy's class, and he got Thomas Scheff, who's apparently a specialist in the sponge toss.

All this trading has got Mrs. Bosh thinking about making some moves of her OWN.

She even gave me the job of scouting kids from some of the other homerooms to see who we should recruit for OUR team.

That's why it stung when Mrs. Bosh traded me and two other kids for Jesse Range, and threw in a pack of dry-erase markers to close the deal.

<u>Thursday</u>

Yesterday was Field Day at school, and it started off with some controversy. Before the first bell, Mr. Ray gave Jesse Range detention just so he could steal Jesse for his team.

So that meant Mr. Ray's team was totally STACKED, and the rest of us didn't stand a chance.

Before Field Day kicked off, Mrs. Epstein gathered our team on the playground to go over strategy and make some last-minute adjustments. But I still couldn't figure out why she wanted me and those other two kids instead of Jesse Range.

I was only signed up for one event, which was the three-legged race. My partner was Madison Burke, who's about a foot taller than me, which made things kind of awkward.

But when the race started, I finally understood Mrs. Epstein's strategy. She didn't trade for me because I'm FAST. She traded for me because I'm LIGHT.

Me and Madison took first place, and our team was off to a good start. But we had a big setback a few minutes later when Marcello Romera rolled an ankle in the sack race. It turns out the lunch ladies had left some POTATOES in a few of the sacks, and I'll bet that wasn't an ACCIDENT.

Marcello was supposed to run the fifty-yard dash next, and all the other kids on our team were in the middle of events. So Mrs. Epstein told me I was gonna have to fill in for him.

I got second-to-last place because I was still kind of banged up from the three-legged race. But I can't really run fast unless I'm MOTIVATED.

The fastest I've ever run was when I got chased by Rodrick after he stepped in dog poop and I laughed at him. I guarantee you if someone had been timing me that day, I would've clocked in at CHEETAH speed.

The only reason I didn't get last place in the fifty-yard dash was because as soon as the race started, Jesse Range fell flat on his face. And when that happened, I figured he must've tripped on his shoelaces or something.

But it turns out he got paid to take a dive, and no one would've found out if Vice Principal Roy hadn't caught him red-handed after the race accepting his payment behind the school.

Jesse didn't want to get suspended, so he gave up the kids who were in on the betting scheme. And those guys had a whole gambling operation running out of the AV closet on the second floor.

The rest of Mr. Ray's team was cheating, too, but that didn't surprise anyone.

Those kids had stored their water balloons in the cafeteria freezer, and the only reason they got CAUGHT is because George Ralston knocked Mikey Ardalla out cold with a bad throw in the balloon toss.

CLONK

Mrs. Bosh's team won beanbag bingo, and that put them ahead in the standings for a while. But then Mr. Chow's team had back-to-back victories in the water-bucket relay and the sponge toss, so then THEY took the lead.

The janitors' team started moving up in the rankings, and they probably would've taken the top spot if Mr. Washington's arms hadn't given out during the wheelbarrow race.

The final event was the tug-of-war, and it came down to Mrs. Bosh's team versus the lunch ladies. I thought Mrs. Bosh's team was gonna win for SURE, but the lunch ladies outlasted them thanks to a solid job of anchoring by Mrs. Frolley.

When we got back to our classrooms after
the competition, we were all bummed that the
cafeteria ladies were the ones to win the day off
from school. And we were nervous because we
heard the janitors were gonna have to fill in for
them during lunch.

TODAY'S SPECIAL: MEAT SURPRISE

But I guess the school knew it was going to be
an ugly scene, so right before the last bell rang,
Vice Principal Roy made an announcement that
EVERYONE would be getting Friday off.

Friday

I was excited about having a whole day where I didn't have to do anything and was looking forward to sleeping in.

But as soon as Mom found out about my day off, she filled it up with a bunch of appointments that she'd been wanting to schedule.

I was in a bad mood all day, but Mom was really chatty. She wanted to know about Field Day and if I had fun. So I told her the truth, which was that it totally STUNK.

Mom said the reason I've never had a good experience with sports is because I've never been part of a team.

But I told her I was on a team for Field Day, and I've been on a bunch of OTHER sports teams, too. So I figured maybe she'd just blocked out those memories like I wish I could.

But Mom said what she's talking about is being part of a REAL team where everyone has your back. She said some of her happiest times as a kid were when she played sports in middle school.

Mom said that what's great about being part of a team is that you learn how to work together, and you can use those skills for the rest of your life, especially in your JOB.

That sounds a little corny to me, but I guess I don't really know how grown-ups act when they're at work.

Mom said she wants me to give team sports one more shot, and if it doesn't work out, she won't bug me about it anymore. So I told her I'd think it over, but really I'm just hoping she forgets in a day or two.

I don't understand why people get so wrapped up in sports, because it seems to me there are more IMPORTANT things in life.

If you can throw a baseball at 100 miles per hour, you'll make millions of dollars and kids will have your poster on their wall.

But if you're the person who ends up curing cancer, you'll be lucky if you get a pat on the back.

I've always wondered how sports got started in the FIRST place. In ancient times, people were always at war, and I guess they decided they needed to figure out a way they could settle their differences without KILLING each other. So someone came up with the idea of sports as a more peaceful solution.

But over time, sports EVOLVED, and nowadays you've got team mascots and cheerleaders and professional athletes.

I've only been to one professional sports match in my life, and that was when my dad took me into the city to watch a football game. To be honest, I don't remember much about the game itself, but I do remember everything ELSE about that day.

Dad didn't want to spend money to park near the stadium, so we ended up about a mile away in a muddy lot. He broke out his portable grill, and we cooked burgers, which was actually kind of fun.

But I drank WAY too much soda, and on our walk to the stadium, I knew I had to find a bathroom or I was gonna wet my pants.

Dad didn't want to stop at one of the porta-
potties because the lines for those were too long.
But I told him I didn't think I could make it all
the way to the stadium, so I begged him to let
me pull over.

I had to wait twenty minutes in line, and finally
it was my turn. But I wished Dad had given me
a little advance warning about what those things
were like inside, because I would've just HELD it.

It was a smart move making that pit stop, though, because when we got to the stadium, there was ANOTHER long line for security. And we missed the whole first quarter of the game waiting to get in.

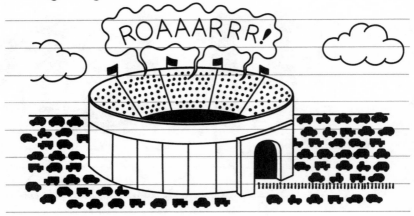

When we finally got inside and found our seats, there were some guys sitting in them. And it took forever to sort THAT out.

I don't know why they even bother to have seats, because no one was SITTING in them anyway. And most of the people in our section were too big for somebody my height to see around.

Since I couldn't see the field, I had no idea what was happening. And Dad was too wrapped up in the game to tell me what was going on.

Eventually I realized I could see the game if I just watched it on the Jumbotron, which is this giant screen that hangs high above the field.

Whenever there was a pause in the action, they turned the cameras on the fans.

They had this thing called "Fan of the Game," where you could win a prize by acting crazy when they put you up on the screen. And some people were really GOING for it.

I knew there was no chance of me winning Fan of the Game if I was behind a bunch of people. So during a time-out, I stepped into the aisle and really hammed it up for the cameras.

But I guess I was embarrassing Dad, so he gave me some money and told me I should go up to the concourse and get some snacks and a souvenir.

I spent my money on popcorn and one of those giant foam fingers. But when I turned to walk away from the souvenir stand, there was a loud noise that shook the whole stadium.

Apparently when the home team scores, they shoot off a CANNON. But I wished Dad had warned me that might happen, because I seriously thought we were in DANGER.

After I was sure the coast was clear, I went to find Dad. But I couldn't remember which section we were sitting in, and Dad was the one who had our tickets.

I started to panic, because there were 80,000 people in that stadium, and everyone looked the same from behind. Plus, the game was tied, and the fans were too distracted to help some lost kid.

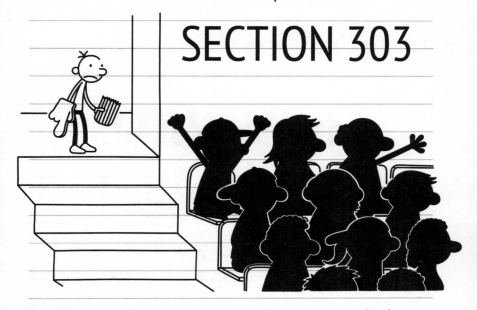

SECTION 303

Luckily an usher saw me wandering around the concourse and brought me to the Child Finder Station.

They asked me a few questions about who I was and where I last saw my father, but by then I was so shook up I could barely even remember my own name.

CHILD FINDER STATION

The next thing I knew, I had a camera in my face and they put me on the Jumbotron.

LOST CHILD

Frank Heffley please come to the Child Finder Station in Concourse B

Then I realized this was my chance to win Fan of the Game, so I made the most of my opportunity.

LOST CHILD

**Frank Heffley
please come
to the Child
Finder Station
in Concourse B**

The good news was that our team won in the last second. The bad news was that Dad didn't get to see it because he had to come get ME. And believe it or not, I DID win Fan of the Game, and we got two free tickets to the NEXT match.

But I don't remember going to another game after that, so I think Dad must've taken Rodrick.

MUNCH
MUNCH

What really stuck with me about that day was how they tried to keep things entertaining for the fans. And I think our church could learn a few lessons from the professional sports experience.

First of all, when they introduce the priest and altar servers, they should dim the lights and play some loud music. Because that would get everyone HYPED.

AND NOW... ALL THE WAY FROM ST. MARY'S SEMINARY IN BALTIMORE...

Another thing they could do is have a mascot to make the service more fun for little kids.

Sometimes you need to break things up to keep people energized, so they could put in a halftime show. And there's all SORTS of crazy stuff you could do for entertainment.

But the biggest upgrade to the church experience would be if they added a JUMBOTRON. For starters, it would help the people in the back feel like they were closer to the action.

They could even have a random drawing to let the people who came in late get a seat up FRONT.

YOU'VE BEEN SELECTED FOR A
PEW UPGRADE!

Plus, they could use the Jumbotron to encourage people to be a little more generous when they pass the donation basket around.

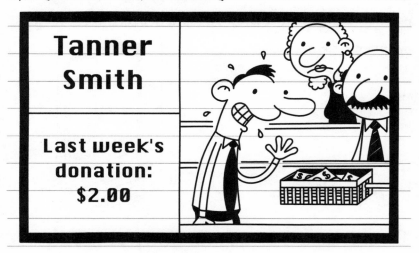

I've got a bunch of OTHER suggestions, and I actually took the time to write them down. But I guess the people who run our church must be pretty busy, because so far nobody's gotten back to me.

Tuesday

I was really hoping Mom would just forget about making me join a team, but she's been pressuring me every single day.

I tried to tell her that in twenty years regular sports will be replaced by e-sports, and athletes won't even have to leave their couches to compete. But I guess she's too old to get excited about what things are gonna be like in the future.

One of the reasons I haven't decided on what sport to play is because I'm not really that GOOD at anything.

I've been racking my brain trying to remember a time when I did something athletic to help figure out which sport is right for me.

And all I can think of was the time at lunch when I landed a balled-up napkin in Justin White's empty milk glass.

When I made that shot, the whole cafeteria went NUTS. And I'm pretty sure it's the biggest athletic achievement of my life.

Some people were even saying they should put a plaque in the spot where I threw the napkin so future students would know about it.

FROM THIS SPOT
Greg Heffley
TOSSED A NAPKIN INTO A GLASS
ON A MOVING TRAY FROM A
DISTANCE OF
25 FEET

For the rest of the year, kids tried to re-create my shot. And that turned the lunch period into a NIGHTMARE.

I thought my napkin shot proved I had some TALENT, and I told Mom maybe I could try out for the basketball team.

Well, that got her all excited, because she said she played basketball when she was my age, and her team was really GOOD. Then she said maybe basketball skills run in our family.

BOUNCE

Mom said her team made it all the way to the state finals one year. But when I asked her what happened in the championship game, she said it wasn't important.

Mom said what mattered was that I'd be a part of a TEAM. Then she went to her computer to figure out how to sign me up to play.

I was glad Mom was excited that I decided on a sport, but there was actually ANOTHER reason I picked basketball.

I heard some kids talking about tryouts at school today, and there are only two teams for my whole grade, with ten players on each one. And if you don't make a team, you get CUT.

I'm sure there will be a lot of kids trying out next week, so I don't stand a CHANCE of making it. And once it's over, I can finally get Mom off my back with this sports stuff.

Sunday

When I got to the gym for basketball tryouts tonight, I counted twenty-eight kids. That meant twenty kids would make one of the two teams, and everyone else would get cut. So I liked my odds.

Plus, most of the kids looked WAY better than me. A lot of these guys have been playing since kindergarten, and they could dribble between their legs and do other crazy stuff with the ball.

BOUNCE

The only real experience I've had with basketball was when we did a basketball unit in Phys Ed last year. And that only lasted two days.

On top of that, the school's only basketball was deflated, and the Phys Ed teacher couldn't find the needle that went with the pump. So we had to use balloons instead.

BOOP

There were a handful of kids at tryouts tonight who didn't look like they were that good, which made me a little nervous.

I was worried I could end up making one of the teams by accident, and then I'd have to play a whole season. So I thought about actually doing badly on PURPOSE, just in case.

But my plan went out the window when Mom came to watch tryouts. Because now I knew I'd have to give it my best effort.

Tryouts started at 7:00 p.m., and they handed each kid a practice jersey with a big number on the front and back. And from the way those things smelled, I'm guessing they've never been WASHED.

They split us up into four groups to do drills in different areas of the gym, and my group started off with dribbling. I was having a little trouble with the hand-eye coordination thing, so I kept dribbling it off my shoe.

I noticed that every time I messed up, some guy with a clipboard would write down my number.

So I tried to stay behind the guys with the clipboards, and the other kids who stunk started copying me.

Every once in a while I'd dribble five or six times in a row, and of course no one was watching THEN. But Mom made sure to let the guys with the clipboards know when I was doing well.

NUMBER EIGHT HASN'T DRIBBLED OFF HIS SHOE IN A WHILE!

After we dribbled with our right hands for a few minutes, the guy in charge of our group said it was time to switch to our LEFT hands. I thought he was joking, and I actually LAUGHED.

HA HA!

But I probably shouldn't have, because that just made him write down my number.

I guess some people can do things with both hands, but not me. In fact, my left hand is practically USELESS.

One time I sprained my right wrist and I had to take a test at school using my left hand. And I think I would've done better if I'd held the pencil in my MOUTH.

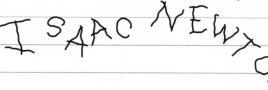

7. Who developed the theory of gravity?

ISAAC NEWTON

Once we finished with our dribbling drills, we switched to free throws. And I really wished I hadn't learned to shoot a basketball with a BALLOON, because I totally misjudged how much effort I needed to put into my shot.

HUP!

I think Mom could see I wasn't doing so great, so whenever one of the evaluators got near her, she'd snitch on the OTHER kids who were struggling.

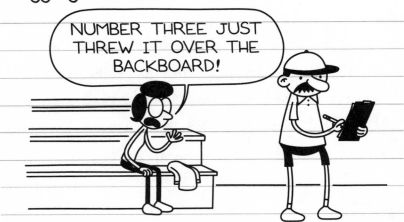

But it's not like Mom was the ONLY parent helping their own kid. Some of the evaluators had kids who were trying out tonight, so I wonder how fair the scoring really was.

By the end of the night, it was pretty obvious
who was gonna make a team and who wasn't. But
I guess they needed to decide which kid was gonna
get the final spot, because they made the bottom
nine kids duke it out in a scrimmage. And all I can
say is it wasn't PRETTY.

Once that was over, they collected our jerseys.
The guy running tryouts told everyone that if we
made a team, our parents would get an e-mail by
tomorrow night. But after that experience, I'm
not exactly holding my BREATH.

Tuesday

When I got home from school yesterday, my plan was to relax and maybe take a nap. So I was pretty surprised when I walked into the kitchen.

I was confused, because I knew for SURE I didn't make either of the basketball teams. But Mom said she heard from one of the coaches who said I DID. Then she showed me the e-mail to prove it.

It was from Mr. Patel, Preet Patel's father. Preet's one of the best athletes in our grade, and during the student-teacher basketball game last year, Preet totally DOMINATED.

I couldn't understand how I got on the same team as a kid like THAT. But Mom said the evaluators must've seen something special in me, and that's why I made the cut.

When I thought back to the night before, I couldn't remember Preet actually being at tryouts. So now I was even MORE confused.

At school today, Jabari Bruce told me what happened. Preet missed tryouts because he had to go to his uncle's funeral, and the rule was that if you skipped tryouts, you couldn't be on a team.

So Mr. Patel made a NEW team with Preet plus all the kids who got cut, just so his son could play this season.

Well, I wasn't happy to hear THAT. I thought I was off the hook for basketball, and now all of a sudden I was on an actual team. And I knew there was no way Mom was letting me out of this, either.

Our first practice was tonight at the elementary school. And when Mr. Patel saw our team assembled for the first time, I'll bet he had second thoughts about taking this on.

My teammates were the kids who were in that last scrimmage at tryouts, and I already knew a few of them from school. Jabari Bruce and Tommy Chu were part of that trade deal with me on Field Day.

JABARI BRUCE

TOMMY CHU

Then there was Darren and Marcus Woodley, who might actually be decent athletes if they weren't always trying to KILL each other.

DARREN WOODLEY

MARCUS WOODLEY

We also had Edward Mealy, who hasn't said a word since second grade, and Kevin Pomodoro, who nobody can understand when he's wearing his retainer.

SPLASKSH?

EDWARD MEALY

KEVIN POMODORO

I guess it's always good to have a little height on your basketball team, so we're lucky to have Yusef Meskin. But Yusef likes to scoop up kids who are my size and put them in "The Cave."

It's also good to have a little TOUGHNESS, and that's where Ruby Bird comes in. And the reason she's on a boys' team is because she attacked one of the evaluators at the GIRLS' tryouts for writing her number down.

Anyway, I wouldn't have blamed Preet or his dad for walking out as soon as they got a good look at us. But Mr. Patel gathered the team around him so he could give a SPEECH.

Mr. Patel said that we might not have the most talented team, but we were going to outwork everyone else in the league. And he said we were gonna learn to play the RIGHT way, starting tonight.

I figured that if this was the guy who taught Preet how to play, maybe he could teach the REST of us, too.

Tommy Chu raised his hand and asked how come we were meeting in the elementary school cafetorium instead of the GYM.

Mr. Patel explained that the two other teams booked all the gym time for the season, so we were gonna have to make do with the LEFTOVERS.

I didn't understand how we were supposed to play basketball when we didn't have a HOOP, but Mr. Patel said that we were gonna start with the fundamentals and work up to shooting later on.

We did some dribbling drills, and then moved on to passing. But with all the tables set up in the cafetorium, there wasn't a lot of room to move around. So half of us had to go on the stage, which was set up for a kindergarten play.

Even though we were trying our hardest, Mr. Patel was getting frustrated we weren't picking things up more quickly. And every time one of us made a mistake, he'd make us run wind sprints to the other side of the cafetorium.

But that just made us tired, so we made even MORE mistakes. And after a while, everyone except Preet was running sprints.

Personally, I don't think coaches should use running as a punishment, because all it does is make kids hate to run.

And I doubt the track coach forces his team to play BASKETBALL whenever they're slacking.

The thing I hate the most about running is that it makes you SWEAT. My theory about sweat is that it's your body's way of telling you you're working too hard, and you need to take it easy. But when I shared my thoughts with Mr. Patel, he just made me run more wind sprints.

When I got in the car after practice, Mom wanted to hear all about it. I told her how our team was basically just Preet and a bunch of scrubs, so we weren't gonna be any good this season.

But Mom said I'd probably get a lot of playing time on this team, which got me WORRIED. Every kid dreams about hitting the big shot to win the game for their team, but there's a FLIP side. And that's being the person who blows it.

There's a guy in my town named Anthony Grow, and twenty years ago he missed a kick on an empty net and lost a game against Slacksville, who's our town's biggest rival.

And now he can't go anywhere without people reminding him about it.

If I was Anthony, I'd just move to Slacksville, because over there he's a HERO.

"The Miss"

I made the mistake of telling Mom how I was worried about messing up like Anthony Grow, and she told me a story that made me feel even MORE nervous about things.

Mom had been the backup point guard on her middle-school basketball team, and in the championship game, the regular point guard got HURT. So with the score tied in the fourth quarter, Mom had to go in and take her place.

Mom said she actually did pretty well, but with the clock winding down she got double-teamed. So she had to heave the ball up at the buzzer, and her shot came up short.

Mom says she's GLAD it happened because it taught her to deal with failure and made her a better person. But I'd be willing to bet Mom's teammates just wished she hadn't CHOKED.

Thursday

I should've done a little more research before I decided on basketball as my sport, because the schedule is BRUTAL.

We've got practice three days a week plus one game on Saturday and another on Sunday. And on top of all that, I'm supposed to keep up with my homework and get enough sleep to make it through school the next day.

It's hard ENOUGH getting sleep with all the racket outside my window every night. And that's because we put up a basketball hoop in our driveway.

THUMP THUMP
THUMP
THUMP

When I made the basketball team, Mom went out
and bought a backboard and hoop for above the
garage. I guess she was hoping I could put up
extra shots on the nights I didn't have practice.

But I haven't taken a single shot on that thing,
because the second it went up, the teenagers in
our neighborhood swooped in.

Ever since they took down the outdoor hoops at our school, there haven't been a lot of places where kids can play. So now they come to our house, and Dad has to park down the street when he gets home from work.

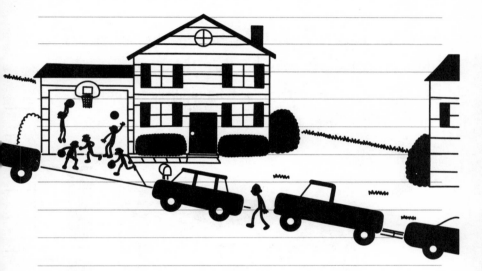

Dad told Mom he wanted to take the hoop down, but Mom said she was happy that kids were outdoors having fun.

I guess I wouldn't have minded too much, either, but the teenagers don't know when to STOP. And when we're heading to bed for the night, those guys are still out there going hard.

Lately, Mom's been trying to give them a hint that it's time to go home by flicking the lights above the garage on and off. But I guess teenagers aren't real good at taking hints, because they just keep right on playing.

So a few nights ago, Mom turned the lights off when it got dark outside. But those guys were PREPARED, and they set up a generator and lights in no time.

RRRRRR

Last night, Dad reached his breaking point and called the COPS, who were at the house ten minutes later.

I thought that would be the end of it, but it turns out cops like basketball, too.

We've kind of given up on trying to stop people from using the hoop. But I guarantee you that the first time there's nobody out there, we're taking that thing down.

Another reason I've been so tired lately is because our practices have been starting at 9:30 p.m. We've been using the elementary school gym, but we have to wait until the other two teams are done with THEIR practices before we can start ours.

On our first night at the gym, Mr. Patel forgot his bag of basketballs and had to go home to get it. And while he was gone, Darren Woodley noticed the Phys Ed closet was open, so we went inside. There was all SORTS of fun equipment in there, like pogo sticks and Hula-Hoops and even a giant parachute.

It had been a long time since any of us had played with that stuff, and all of a sudden we were like little kids again.

We even made up a whole new game that used those square four-wheeled scooters and some giant plastic bowling pins. And it was actually WAY more fun than basketball.

But when Mr. Patel came back with the bag of balls, he shut our game down.

Mr. Patel told us we were there to play basketball, not to goof around. Then he made us put everything back in the closet where we found it.

I've read that basketball started off with a bunch of guys horsing around with a leather soccer ball and a peach basket, and now it's popular all over the WORLD. But if their coach had been anything like Mr. Patel, it probably never would've happened.

DOINK

And I'll bet Mr. Patel's gonna feel pretty dumb when the sport we invented goes PRO.

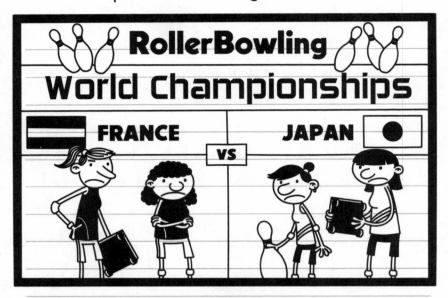

Once we finished putting all the equipment back in the closet, Mr. Patel lined us up at the foul line to practice free throws. And even after he showed us the right way to shoot, most of us couldn't get the hang of it.

After missing a bunch of times in a row, I was getting pretty frustrated. So I shot the ball BACKWARD, just for kicks. And believe it or not, it went IN.

My teammates were pretty impressed, and after that, EVERYONE tried making a backward shot.

But Mr. Patel shut THAT down, too.

He said we were never gonna improve until we started taking things more SERIOUSLY. I tried to explain that I was better at shooting backward than forward, and maybe the way he was teaching us was all wrong.

But I guess Mr. Patel thought I was being a smart aleck, so he made me run wind sprints until the end of practice.

On the first few nights we just worked on stuff like dribbling, passing, and shooting. But at the beginning of last night's practice, Mr. Patel said we were gonna SCRIMMAGE.

Everybody was pretty excited that we were finally gonna get to actually PLAY. But right when we were about to start, a group of men my dad's age walked into the gym.

One of the guys walked up to Mr. Patel and said we were gonna have to get off the court because the Men's League had the gym booked at 9:30 every Wednesday night.

But Mr. Patel said that we had the gym until 10:30, and he had double-checked with the rec department that afternoon.

Things started to get a little HEATED, but then Mr. Patel came up with a solution. He said we could play those guys in a scrimmage, and whoever won could have the court.

I was a little nervous about playing a group of grown men. But these guys didn't look like they were in the best shape, and I thought we might be able to take them.

It took a long time for the Men's League to warm up. I thought they were getting cold feet and were just STALLING.

After those guys finally finished stretching, we got started. We won the tip-off, and I figured we were on our way to an easy win. But it was all downhill after that.

Those Men's League guys might not have been
super athletic, but they knew how to PLAY. And
they totally made fools out of us.

The whole time, they never stopped TALKING.
And I hate to admit it, but they were really
getting inside our HEADS.

It was all corny stuff that only grown-ups would
say, but it really worked. And the more they
talked, the more we struggled.

123

The person who was getting the most frustrated was PREET. And I could tell he really wanted to stick it to these guys.

But they had figured out that Preet was our only good player, and whenever he'd get the ball, they were all over him.

At one point, Preet stole the ball and sprinted to the other end of the court for what should've been an easy layup. I think Preet wanted to make a statement, because he decided to DUNK it.

We were all pretty excited to see Preet throw it down. But I guess he needs to grow a few more inches before he's ready for that.

Preet landed awkwardly on his ankle. And even though the game wasn't officially over, I think the Men's League saw it as a WIN.

I thought Preet just rolled his ankle and he'd be back to normal for the next practice. But when he showed up at the gym tonight, he was on CRUTCHES.

It turns out Preet BROKE his ankle, and he's out for the whole season. And that's bad news for the rest of us, because without him we're toast.

It's even worse news for Mr. Patel, because now he's stuck coaching this team for the rest of the season. And I'm sure he'd rather be spending his free time watching TV or learning to juggle.

But at the beginning of practice, Mr. Patel gave a speech. He said injuries are a part of the game, and the rest of us were gonna have to step up.

Then he ran us through some plays that were supposed to make it easy to score. We started with five on three, but nobody could make a basket. So we went to five on two, and then five on one, and we STILL couldn't score.

We finally hit a shot when it was five on ZERO, but the play didn't go the way Mr. Patel drew it up. So if we actually score in our first game this weekend, it's gonna be by blind LUCK.

At the end of practice, Mr. Patel said he had a
surprise for us, and opened a big cardboard box.
Then he started handing out UNIFORMS.

I noticed the uniforms looked kind of familiar,
and I recognized the SMELL, too. Mr. Patel
explained that there wasn't enough time to get
new uniforms for the team, so they had to recycle
the ones from tryouts.

But there was something DIFFERENT about the jerseys, because now there was a logo printed on the back.

Mr. Patel told us that every team has a sponsor to help pay for stuff like gym rentals, and our sponsor for the season was Marconi's Sub Shop. I guess it was tough finding a good sponsor, because I'm pretty sure Marconi's is still closed for health code violations.

Saturday

Today was our first game of the season, and it was at the elementary school gym. Coach Patel asked everyone to get there a half hour early so we could go over the plan and warm up.

Mr. Patel showed us a few new plays he designed, which looked like they must've taken all night to draw up. I just hoped the other guys on the team understood what all the little symbols were supposed to mean, because it was complete gibberish to ME.

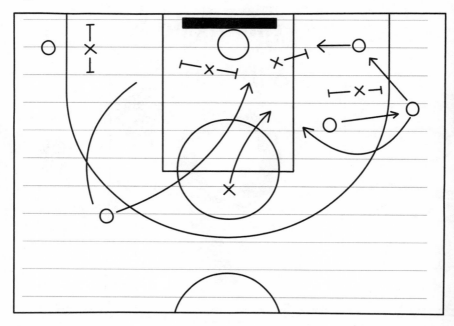

While we were going over the plays, the stands started filling up. I was nervous to play in front of a crowd, but it turns out I didn't need to worry about it. Because when Coach Patel put in his starting lineup, I wasn't in it.

We were playing against Franklin, which is a town that's twenty minutes down the road from us. Things got off to a rocky start when Franklin won the opening tip-off and took it all the way down to the other end for a layup. And that set the tone for the rest of the game.

Kevin Pomodoro was our point guard, because he's the only kid on our team who can dribble while looking up. But Kevin was basically playing one-handed, because every time he needed to yell out one of Coach Patel's plays, he'd have to take his retainer out so people could understand him.

Eventually the Franklin players caught on, and whenever Kevin would call a play, they'd go for the steal.

Our team was trying its best to follow Coach Patel's new plays, but I don't think anyone knew who was an X and who was an O, so it was just pure confusion out there.

Coach Patel started yelling at the kids on the bench like what was happening out there was OUR fault. And I just acted like I was ashamed because it seemed like that's what he was looking for.

Coach Patel started subbing kids out of the game, and I was getting worried he was gonna put ME in. So I moved to the end of the bench and just prayed he'd forget I was there.

But Mom was in the stands, and she wasn't exactly helping.

PUT GREG IN!

Even though the elementary school gym is our home court, it's not like we have a home court ADVANTAGE. First of all, the gym is about seventy years old, and there are all sorts of dead spots on the floor. So even when someone on our team would try to get something going, they'd end up losing their dribble.

Plus, there's bubble gum and other crud caked on the floor. And on a fast break, Jabari Bruce actually lost a shoe running down the court.

Whoever designed the gym did a lousy job, because there's no room between the sidelines and the walls. So anyone trying to save a ball from going out of bounds is risking their LIFE.

On top of that, the doors to the restrooms are close to the baseline. And in the first quarter, there was a line for the ladies' room.

To make matters worse, the guys who used the men's room kept leaving the door open. And at one point someone threw a bad pass and the ball landed in the URINAL.

One of the refs washed the ball off in the sink and then dried it with some paper towels. I don't know what they pay those guys, but whatever it is it's not ENOUGH.

Believe it or not, my team managed to score a handful of buckets. But when the buzzer went off, the score was 38—6. I was just glad that Coach Patel didn't put me in, because if he had, I guarantee we would've lost by even MORE.

I've played enough sports to know that when the game's over, you're supposed to shake hands with the other team and say it was a good game. So that's exactly what I DID.

But I wished someone had told me we were only at HALFTIME, because maybe then I wouldn't have made such a fool of myself.

Coach Patel told us to meet in the locker room so we could get ready for the second half. But the elementary school didn't HAVE a locker room, so we had to settle for the men's bathroom. And unfortunately it was occupied, so we didn't even have it all to ourselves.

But that didn't stop Coach Patel from launching into his halftime speech as soon as he stepped in the room. I was a little bummed out that Coach was making us listen to a speech at halftime. Because if you ask me, I think halftime should be a VACATION from the game.

But Coach Patel started by going over everything we were doing wrong, and all the adjustments we needed to make in the second half if we wanted to win.

Then he told us a story about this group of Scottish warriors from a long time ago. He said they were surrounded by their enemies and were totally outnumbered, but they won the battle by sticking together and fighting with everything they had.

He said if we followed the game plan, maybe WE could get a victory, too. And I have to admit, it was a pretty good speech, because by the time we left that bathroom we were ready to go to WAR.

There were still a few minutes to go before the second half started, so everyone used the chance to rehydrate.

The Woodleys were responsible for supplying the drinks for the first game, so we all helped ourselves to bottles of water from the cooler.

But I guess the Woodleys never cleaned out their cooler from summer vacation, because there were some LEFTOVERS in there, too.

There were even a half-filled bottle of ketchup and a full bottle of mustard in the cooler, but Yusef and Ruby weren't too choosy about their refreshments.

I guess they figured they'd take every bit of fuel they could GET.

142

Coach kept Yusef in for the whole first half,
and he was so sweaty that he had to wring out
his jersey. But I wished he hadn't wrung it out
into the COOLER, because there were still some
bottles of water in there.

Like I said, everyone was fired up after that
speech by Coach Patel. But I guess those guys in
Scotland had something we DIDN'T, because the
second half of the game started off a lot like the
FIRST.

Things got so out of control in the fourth quarter that Coach Patel put me and the rest of the bench in. But if he was hoping we'd give our team a spark and turn things around, he must've been pretty disappointed.

To be honest, I can't even remember what the final score was. All I remember was that on the ride home, Mom said our coach should've run different plays, and that I should've got more playing time.

The only thing Dad said was that if this was GOLF we would've won, because we had the lowest score. I guess they were both trying to make me feel better, but it didn't really work.

<u>Sunday</u>

Mom's always saying how sports brings people together, but I think she might actually be wrong about that. Because in my experience, sports just tears us APART.

The people in my town don't like the surrounding towns because they always beat us in sports. But the town we hate the most is Slacksville, because those guys always DESTROY us.

It's been going on like this since before I was born. And whenever an old-timer in my town mentions Slacksville, they always spit.

My town's issues with Slacksville go a lot deeper than SPORTS, though. About a hundred years ago, we were supposed to get a jewelry factory in our town, which would've brought in a lot of jobs and money. But some bigwigs from Slacksville swooped in at the last minute and stole the factory from us.

These days, Slacksville's got ALL the good stuff, like a mall and two golf courses. And all we've got to show for ourselves is an abandoned drive-in movie theater and Marconi's Sub Shop.

So we're always looking for ways to get back at those guys. And since we can't beat them in sports, we have to be CREATIVE.

Last year, the state was planning on putting a big garbage dump in our town. But we made some changes to our zoning laws, so the state had to put the dump in Slacksville instead. And I've heard they're not too HAPPY about it, either.

It seemed like things were gonna change a few months back when the mayor of Slacksville called our mayor saying he wanted to make a peace offering. Every year, our town has a giant bonfire in the park on the Fourth of July, and this year the people of Slacksville wanted to donate the wood.

The timing was great, because our town was out of money for recreational stuff and couldn't afford to do the bonfire this year anyway.

So our mayor gave the plan the green light, and a few days later trucks started showing up from Slacksville with piles of lumber. And they even set it all up for FREE.

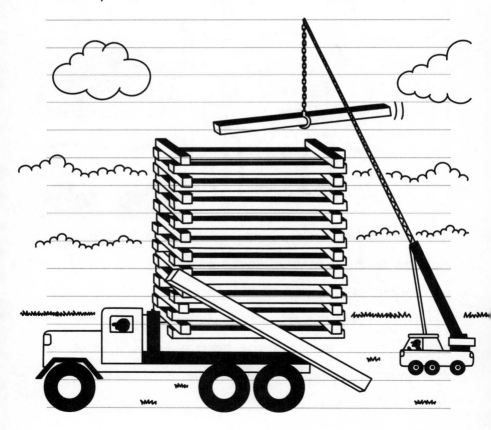

But right before we lit the fire on the Fourth of July, our health inspector came by the town park and said the wood from Slacksville was chemically treated, so we couldn't burn it because it would release dangerous fumes into the air.

The next day, our mayor called the mayor of Slacksville and told him he'd have to send someone to haul the wood away. But I guess their mayor already knew the wood was full of chemicals and thought the whole thing was pretty hilarious.

TOWN OF
SLACKSVILLE

So now we've got a giant pile of rotting lumber in the middle of our town park, and this fall the preschoolers had to play their soccer games AROUND it.

BOOP

But their soccer season got cut short when a bunch of animals moved into the woodpile, and everyone agreed it was too dangerous for kids to keep playing near it.

So I guess Slacksville has the last laugh, at least for now.

The reason I'm bringing this stuff up is because today was our first away game, and of course it was in Slacksville. I got a queasy feeling when we drove past the sign, because I hadn't been there in YEARS.

Our game was at Slacksville High, and their gym was WAY better than ours. The court looked brand new, and I didn't see a single piece of gum on the floor.

The gym was packed before we got there, and people started booing during warm-ups.

BOOOOOOOOOO!

THOOMP

Only a few of our parents showed up to cheer us on. I had to carpool to the game with Edward Mealy, because Mom said she needed to go with Dad to Manny's preschool play.

But I kind of wonder if Mom bailed on me because she knew what was in store for our team in Slacksville.

I was pretty anxious for the game to get started so I could take my spot at the end of the bench. But there were already people sitting in that spot, and there wasn't any room for ME.

There was an empty space a few rows up in the stands, so when the game started, that's where I went. But I was afraid people were gonna notice that I wasn't from Slacksville and give me a hard time. So whenever the crowd booed my team, I did, too.

It was actually pretty easy to do, because we got off to another terrible start. Slacksville started the game by hitting a deep three-pointer, and then they stole the ball and hit ANOTHER one. And before long, they were ahead by twenty points.

I thought that once they built up a lead they'd start to take it easy on us. But I guess everyone in Slacksville is still sore over the garbage dump, because they never let up.

They started running a full-court press, which meant we couldn't even get the ball past half-court. In fact, we couldn't even get the ball in play because those Slacksville kids were all OVER us.

Coach Patel was yelling at our team from the sidelines. But his voice was drowned out by the Slacksville crowd.

Every once in a while my team would get the ball inbounds, but then three or four Slacksville players would swarm the kid who got the pass.

And we couldn't even get any rebounds, because their center was so big he actually made Yusef look SMALL.

By halftime, the score was 52–0, and I was hoping the refs would use the mercy rule and end the game. But I guess they don't do that kind of thing in basketball.

TRUDGE

TRUDGE

I'm pretty sure the people who run the Slacksville gym turned up the heat in the visitors' locker room just to make us uncomfortable, because it was like a SAUNA in there.

PANT, PANT!

GASP!

FSSSS

Coach Patel gave another speech, but this one wasn't about Scottish armies or anything like that. It was about PRIDE.

He said that when we stepped onto the floor, we were representing our TOWN. Then he said we shouldn't even look at the score, because the only thing that mattered now was how hard we FOUGHT.

And that got everyone just as fired up as the speech in our first game.

But a few kids on my team took Coach Patel too LITERALLY. Because when the second half started, our team was ready to fight for REAL. Yusef got things started by throwing an elbow, then Ruby Bird took down Slacksville's center.

Then the Woodley brothers started going at it with each OTHER for some reason.

But the refs had BIGGER problems to deal with. Kevin Pomodoro's mother and one of the Slacksville moms started arguing in the stands, and the next thing you knew they were throwing haymakers.

PUNCH

The refs went into the bleachers to break it up, so I decided to make myself some room on the bench, because it was a lot SAFER there.

But I wished I had stayed where I was, because when Ruby and Yusef got ejected for fighting, the coach put me in the game along with Tommy Chu.

The Slacksville coach pulled his starters to give them a rest, and he put in his bench players, too.

Coach Patel told our team to run one of the plays he taught us at practice. And believe it or not, the play actually WORKED.

Now the score was 52–2, and the Slacksville crowd was really annoyed because they thought they were gonna SKUNK us.

So the Slacksville coach put all his starters back in the game. They reeled off twenty-three straight points, and it seemed like there was nothing we could do to stop them.

I didn't understand any of Coach Patel's plays, so I just ran up and down the court and tried to look like I knew what I was doing. But then Kevin got double-teamed, and he threw the ball to ME.

I didn't know WHAT I was supposed to do, so I just tried to throw the ball to get RID of it. But a Slacksville player hacked me on the arm and the ref called a foul.

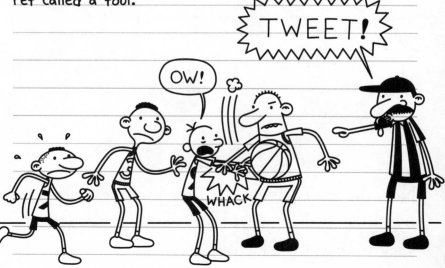

The ref put me at the free throw line and gave me the ball. And I really wished I remembered the stuff Coach Patel taught us about shooting technique, because everyone's eyes were on me.

And the Slacksville crowd wasn't exactly making it easy to CONCENTRATE.

I think fans should have to be QUIET when a player's trying to shoot a free throw, but when I tried to get them to be more respectful, it didn't work.

I totally whiffed my shot, and the crowd let me hear about it. But at least it was OVER.

Then the ref gave me the ball and told me to shoot AGAIN. I thought he was just being nice by giving me another try, but it turns out that when there's a shooting foul, you get TWO shots.

I didn't want to miss AGAIN, so I thought about shooting it backward to at least have a CHANCE of making it. But I didn't wanna make Coach Patel mad, and decided to try a granny shot, where you throw the ball from between your legs.

But when I airballed that one, even the GRANNIES laughed at me.

BWAHAHAHA!

HUP!

After that, I was ready to go back to my spot on the bench. So I subbed myself out of the game, which I found out later is not actually a thing a player is supposed to do.

MEALY! YOU'RE UP!

Slacksville kept running up the score, and before long it was 98—2. Then one of their players hit a three-pointer, so now they had 101 points. But the scoreboard could only display two digits for each team, so all of a sudden it looked like we were AHEAD.

So we started going CRAZY on the bench, and that really ticked off the Slacksville crowd.

The clock was winding down, and Slacksville tried to move the ball up the court. But now our team was playing with PRIDE, and we locked it down on the defensive end.

Slacksville managed to get past us, and they hit a layup. So when the final buzzer went off, they had LAPPED us.

The only thing that made me feel better was when Mr. Mealy stopped at the Slacksville dump to get rid of an old mattress. We might not ever beat those guys in sports, but at least our town doesn't SMELL.

STATE DU

<u>Tuesday</u>

I wish I could say that after Slacksville our team got better and we won a few games during the season, but that's not what happened. In fact, things just got worse and worse as the season went on.

After the Slacksville game, Mr. Marconi from Marconi's Sub Shop called Coach Patel and told him he didn't want to sponsor our team anymore. But by then it was too late to change our uniforms, so we just used electrical tape to black out the logos.

And that turned into a problem, because in our next game one of the kids on the other team got electrical tape from Yusef's jersey stuck to his face. Then when the kid's mom removed the tape, she pulled his eyebrow clean OFF.

Whenever we'd start to fall behind in a game, Mom would let Coach Patel know what he should be doing differently. And I'm not sure he really appreciated her advice.

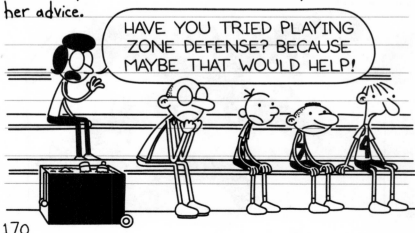

HAVE YOU TRIED PLAYING ZONE DEFENSE? BECAUSE MAYBE THAT WOULD HELP!

Somewhere along the line, the other teams' coaches started feeling SORRY for us, so they'd play their benchwarmers instead of their starters. But that didn't change the RESULTS.

The parents on our team started complaining to the rec league that we were losing by too many points, and it wasn't good for our self-esteem. So the league made some rule changes to help keep things under control.

The new rules said that if your team was ahead by twenty or more points, you had to pass five times before you took a shot.

And that did actually keep the score down, but it was pretty humiliating when the kids on the other team counted their passes out LOUD.

Then teams started trying to keep their scores down on their OWN. And they tried all sorts of things, like only dribbling with their left hands and even closing their eyes when they shot.

But the scores were STILL lopsided, so halfway through the season the rec league did something a little more drastic to help us win. One weekend they dropped us down a whole age group, and the week after that they dropped us down ANOTHER level.

And there's nothing like having your butt handed to you by a bunch of elementary school kids to make you feel good about yourself.

I only made one basket the entire season, but it was on the wrong hoop. And I guess Coach Patel wanted me to have my moment, so he didn't even say anything when it happened.

By the end of the season, only Mom and a few other parents came to the games. And by then even the REFS weren't paying attention.

We were so happy when the season finally ended that we gave Coach Patel one of those victory baths like they do when a team wins a championship. But I hope he took a REAL shower when he got home, because that thing was full of SWEAT.

After our last game, we had an end-of-season banquet at Marconi's Sub Shop. And the only reason Mr. Marconi agreed to host it was because his restaurant still wasn't officially open and he needed the business. But I avoided any food with mayonnaise in it, just in case.

Coach Patel handed out awards, and every player got one. But since no one was any GOOD this season, he had to get creative.

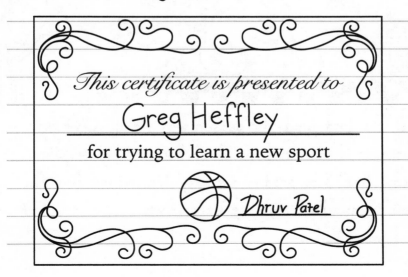

This certificate is presented to

Greg Heffley

for trying to learn a new sport

Dhruv Patel

After we had cake, Coach Patel gave a speech. He said that we might not have won any games, but he was proud of us for trying our hardest and never giving up.

Then he said that even though there probably weren't any future professional athletes on our team, there were a lot of OTHER exciting careers out there, like accounting and web design and puppetry.

It wasn't as inspiring as some of the other speeches he gave during the season, but I guess they can't all be winners.

I was just glad the season was finally OVER, because it meant I could go back to my regular life. And I'm pretty sure my teammates felt the same way. But the one person who couldn't let it go was MOM.

Before Mr. Patel got in his car to leave, Mom told him about this state tournament for teams that hadn't won any games during the season. Then she showed him a flyer she'd printed out.

TOUGH SEASON?

Turn that frown upside down in the

SECOND CHANCE TOURNAMENT!

Because there's a winner in everyone!

I really wished Mom had asked me about this FIRST, because the last thing I wanted was to play more BASKETBALL. But luckily Mr. Patel felt the same way.

Mr. Patel told Mom that our team was hopeless at basketball and he wasn't willing to put us through any more misery. And even though it sounded a little harsh, Mom didn't argue with him.

A week later, Mom invited the whole team to our house. I thought this was one of those end-of-the-season parties where you have pizza and maybe watch a movie or something, but it was a whole other THING.

Once everyone got to our house, Mom said she had an announcement to make. She said she was going to enter us in the Second Chance Tournament and that SHE was gonna be our coach.

Then she said we were going to enter the
tournament as a whole new team for a fresh start,
and she started handing out uniforms.

Everyone got kind of excited, because these
uniforms looked EXPENSIVE. The jerseys had
blue-and-gold stitching, and each kid's last name
was written on the back. There was no sponsor
this time, so I'm guessing Mom paid for these out
of her own pocket.

On the front of each jersey was the picture of one of those sled dogs you see in Alaska. And Mom explained that our team was gonna be the HUSKIES, just like her middle-school basketball team.

It was pretty obvious Mom was just trying to relive her glory days through US, but I didn't really care. Because like I said, those uniforms were NICE.

Mom said that this time around we were gonna be WINNERS. And that sounded a whole lot better than being accountants and puppeteers.

Thursday

The big tournament is less than a week away, so our team doesn't have a ton of time to prepare. But after our first practice, I'm kind of glad we DON'T.

Mom's coaching style is completely different from Mr. Patel's. Instead of working on our basketball skills, we did a bunch of touchy-feely team-building exercises.

I just hope Mom knows what she's doing, because I don't see how that stuff is gonna help us win any games.

OK, ALL TOGETHER NOW!
"I'VE GOT YOUR BACK!"

One of the exercises was supposed to help us get to know each other better. We stood in a circle, and when you threw the ball to another player, you had to tell everyone something about yourself. So when it was my turn to throw the ball, I said that I liked mint chocolate chip ice cream.

But when Edward Mealy got the ball, he finally started TALKING. He told us how his stepmom is really strict and how she doesn't like his pet turtle that he got for his birthday.

In fact, he went on for so long that Mom had to take the ball from him and hand it to someone else.

After that, we played some actual basketball. Mom tried teaching us a few plays that her team used the year they reached the state finals, but we were having trouble getting the hang of things.

I didn't think the fact that we were terrible was such a BAD thing. I've seen a bunch of those movies about teams who are underdogs, but then they pull together and win in the end. And I've been wondering if WE could do that.

But the players who are on those teams never make any money, because they're not the ones telling the story. So I've been thinking that if we turn into one of those teams that inspires a movie, I'M gonna be the one to cash in.

So before practice tonight I put together a
permission form and got my teammates to sign it.

I _____ hereby authorize
Greg Heffley to use my likeness and image in
a film or television series and any subsequent
sequels, throughout the universe and in
perpetuity.

SIGN HERE

The only person who gave me an issue about it was
Yusef, who said he'd have to ask his parents before
he could sign the form. But after I promised to
give him my lunch snacks for the next three days,
he was on board, too.

SCRIBBLE
SCRIBBLE

All we need to do NOW is win this tournament so I can sell the rights to one of those studios that makes feel-good movies. And I can already see the poster in my head.

The Second Chance Tournament was halfway across the state. I guess my teammates' parents were burned out on basketball, because none of them wanted to make the drive.

So yesterday Mom rented a big van to get the team to the tournament. She said there was a chance we'd play for two days, so everyone had to pack an overnight bag.

Some kids packed WAY too much for one night. Yusef brought two loaves of bread and a bunch of supplies for sandwiches, plus a backpack filled with chocolate-covered raisins.

186

Jabari brought his video game system and a computer monitor so we could all play games in the van. But I guess it was too much for the vehicle's electrical system to handle, because we had to pull into a repair shop when the circuit board got overloaded.

We made another pit stop when Yusef needed to use the restroom after eating half of the chocolate-covered raisins all by himself. And even though we left two hours earlier than we needed to, we barely made it to the tournament on time.

Since this was a big competition, I thought it would be held at a college campus or a convention center or something.

So I was pretty disappointed when we pulled up at the old prison that's scheduled to be torn down next year.

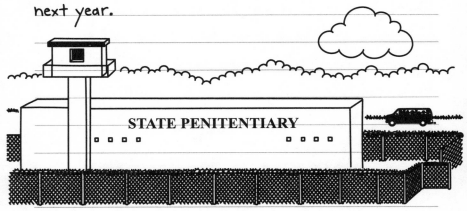

But I guess that's just the way it is when your team is one of the worst in the state.

When Mom went to the desk to register, she got some bad news. There was already a team called the Huskies in the tournament, so she had to come up with ANOTHER name. And I guess Mom was feeling stressed that we were late, so she just wrote down the first name that popped into her head.

SECOND CHANCE
TOURNAMENT
REGISTRATION FORM
Team name: _Winter Dogs_

But when I saw the names of some of the OTHER teams we were competing against, I didn't feel so bad about ours.

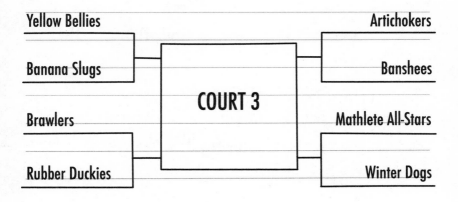

Yellow Bellies

Banana Slugs

Brawlers

Rubber Duckies

COURT 3

Artichokers

Banshees

Mathlete All-Stars

Winter Dogs

The games were being held in a big open area that must've been used as a cafeteria when the prison was open. There was a sign with a list of rules written on it, and I'm not sure if it was for US or for the prisoners.

MESS HALL RULES

1. No sharp objects
2. No swearing
3. No complaining
4. No food fights

The courts were side by side, which meant there wasn't any room for fans to watch the games. But that was OK, because it looked like nobody ELSE'S parents had come to this thing, either.

Our opponents were already warming up on Court Three. And I have to admit, I was a little relieved that we were playing the Mathlete All-Stars in round one.

But I shouldn't have underestimated them, because these guys made up for their lack of basketball skills with their BRAINS.

Their team was lousy on defense, so we scored a bunch, too. But we couldn't do anything to stop their OFFENSE, and at the final buzzer the score was 37—30, Mathlete All-Stars.

Me and my teammates were pretty bummed out because we knew this was our big chance to finally get a win, and we blew it. Plus, we felt a little dumb for packing overnight bags.

But then Mom told us something that was pretty shocking. She said that in the Second Chance Tournament, you played until you WON.

That meant the Mathletes were going home, and we were STAYING.

Well, that changed EVERYTHING. It meant we were actually STUCK in this place until we got a victory. And now it made sense why they decided to hold this tournament in a PRISON.

Mom checked the results for the first-round games to see who we were facing next. The name of the team was the Brawlers, which sounded a little more intimidating than the Mathletes.

But then Mom got the scoop. The Brawlers was a team made up of all the kids in the state who got thrown out of games for FIGHTING, so I guess the "second chance" thing wasn't just about WINS.

When we got our first look at these guys, we knew we were in trouble.

I was glad Mom didn't put me in the starting lineup, because the game was a fight from start to finish. Right after the tip-off, one of the Brawlers clotheslined Kevin. So Ruby Bird jumped on that kid's BACK, and then EVERYONE joined in.

I don't think the refs wanted to get in the middle of a fight, so they just let it go. And I'm pretty sure they didn't blow their whistles ONCE.

Since there wasn't a lot of actual basketball being played, it was a low-scoring contest. But the Brawlers edged us out in the end, and the final score was 6—5.

Our team was pretty gassed from playing two games in a row, but we weren't done yet. We had to face a team called the Stage Whisperers in the third round, and they looked tired, too.

I couldn't figure out what the deal with these guys was until we started playing. They must've been a part of the theater group at their school, because they were all great ACTORS.

Every time one of our players would get anywhere NEAR one of those guys, they'd flop and act like they were injured. And even though we never touched them, we picked up fifteen personal fouls in the first quarter.

Their team scored almost all of their points from the free throw line, and we ended up losing that one 33–17. And if we had to play another game after that, I don't think we could've actually done it.

Luckily the next round wasn't until the morning, so we went to a hotel a few miles away, where I was looking forward to getting a good night's sleep. But I guess Mom didn't think we'd still be playing this late in the tournament, so she hadn't booked our rooms ahead of time. And by then there were only two left in the hotel.

So Mom booked one room for her and Ruby, and one for the REST of us. I don't know what it was like to share a room with Ruby, but I can tell you it sure wasn't fun sharing a room with the guys on my team.

From the way my teammates were acting, I doubt any of those guys had ever been in a hotel room before. And I actually thought about calling security on them a bunch of times.

But I DIDN'T, and that was a big mistake. Because one of them started an ice cube fight and hit a sprinkler in the ceiling.

It turns out that when the sprinklers go off, it triggers the fire alarm.

So we spent the next two hours outside in the freezing cold, along with everyone ELSE who was staying at the hotel, while the fire department reset the alarms.

CHATTER
CHATTER

In the morning, Mom was pretty annoyed with us, but she seemed focused on the day ahead.

During breakfast, Mom said we were heading into the Final Four, and that we all needed to play as a team to pull out a win today.

Then she told everyone about how it felt to lose her very last game, and that she sometimes wonders if she could've done anything DIFFERENT to change the outcome. Mom said she didn't want US to have any regrets, so we needed to leave everything on the floor today.

It was a good speech and all, but the difference between Mom's team and our team was that her team was trying to prove they were the BEST, and we were just trying not to be the WORST. So the truth is, we didn't really need the extra motivation.

Yesterday morning, when we showed up at the tournament, nobody knew who we were. But after setting off the fire alarm last night, EVERYONE did.

And the team we played in the next round was out for REVENGE. They were the only all-girl team in the whole tournament, and I guess they didn't appreciate having their sleep interrupted. So when we faced off against the Banshees, they were ready to PLAY.

TIP

In the third quarter, Mom had to take Ruby out of the game to give her a rest. But I really wished she hadn't put ME in to take her place, because it was like throwing raw meat to a bunch of WOLVES.

I don't even remember what the final score was. All I know is that we lost, and they got to go home.

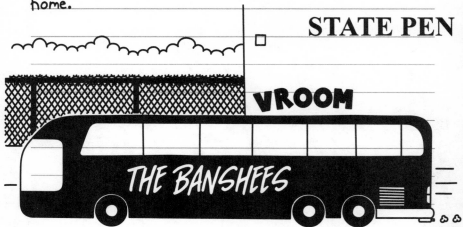

I have no idea how the Banshees lasted so long in the tournament without a win, because those girls were TOUGH. But when I saw the two teams who were still fighting for the chance to go home, I could see why those guys were still here.

The two teams left were the original Huskies and the Funky Dunkers. And they both looked equally terrible to ME, so it was anyone's game to lose.

But the Funky Dunkers only had five players with no subs. So even though they put up a good fight, they ran out of gas at the end. And that meant they had to face us in the FINALS.

I should've figured this out a lot sooner, but EVERYONE in this tournament couldn't go home a winner. And whoever lost the last game would know for sure that they were the worst team in the state.

So we all wanted to win the last game, but nobody wanted it more than MOM. And before we started, she went over the game plan and made some last-minute changes to the lineup.

By that point, almost everybody had left the building, and the place was practically EMPTY. But then two people walked in through the doors.

COURT 1

CLOMP

Preet was wearing some sort of boot, so I guess that meant he didn't need crutches anymore.

Mom asked Mr. Patel what they were doing here, and he said they heard we were playing today, so they came to support us.

But Mom said we didn't need cheerleaders, we needed PLAYERS. Then she asked Preet if he'd be willing to play in his boot. And I guess Preet must've missed competing, because he said YES.

Luckily, Mom had a spare jersey in her bag, and she gave it to Preet to suit up. Then she put him in the starting lineup and told us she was making one more change to the playbook.

Mom threw out all of our plays and replaced them with just one, which was called "Get the Ball to Preet." And everyone was happy because we finally had a play we could UNDERSTAND.

The ref blew the whistle to start the game, and we won the opening tip-off. Yusef passed the ball to Preet, who was better on ONE leg than the rest of us on TWO.

FWIP

TOSS

The only problem was that he couldn't RUN. And every time he scored, the Funky Dunkers got an easy basket at the other end of the floor.

Just before halftime, something really AWFUL happened. A bunch of kids on the other team were trying to stop Preet from shooting, and he stepped on their point guard's foot with his boot.

The kid had to be helped off the floor by his coach and another player, and we all clapped, because for some reason that's what you're supposed to do in that situation.

But now the Funky Dunkers were down to four
players. The head ref said that since the Funky
Dunkers didn't have a full team, they were gonna
have to FORFEIT. And I think their coach was
totally fine with that.

But Mom WASN'T. She said if we were gonna
win, she wanted us to do it fair and square. So
she said she'd send one of OUR players to the
other team so we could finish the game.

I guess the other coach figured he had nothing
to lose, so he agreed. Then he said he'd take
PREET. But the head ref said MOM should be
the one to decide which player to send to the
other team. And after thinking it over for a
minute, she picked ME.

To be honest, I was kind of shocked, because I never expected to get traded by my own MOTHER. But as I walked toward the other team's bench, she whispered something in my ear.

YOU'RE MY SECRET WEAPON!

Well, now I was TOTALLY confused. I wanted our team to win this game just as much as Mom did, but I didn't think she'd want me to CHEAT. I was willing to do whatever it took, though, including putting on someone else's UNIFORM.

When the second half started, I got out on the floor and acted like I was trying my hardest. But I guess my new teammates didn't trust me, anyway, because they wouldn't pass the ball to me.

PASS

After a few minutes, I just stood in the corner to stay out of everyone's way. And that was actually a great spot to watch the game, which was starting to get really GOOD.

Every time Preet would hit some crazy shot, somebody on the Funky Dunkers would score at the other end. It went back and forth like that for the whole second half, and I was so caught up watching the game I forgot I was actually IN it.

So when Preet missed a three-pointer and the ball bounced off the rim, I was shocked when it came to ME.

I didn't know if I should pass or dribble or WHAT. But I couldn't really do anything anyway, because all of a sudden my former teammates were all OVER me.

The clock was ticking down, and the Funky Dunkers were behind by two. So I looked over at the bench to see what Mom wanted me to do, but she didn't exactly look like she was rooting for me.

That's when I realized why Mom sent me to the other side in the first place. It wasn't because I was some sort of "secret weapon." It was because I STUNK, and she knew I'd blow it for the other team.

But by then I honestly didn't CARE. I just wanted to get rid of the ball to give myself a little space.

So I chucked it with all my might.

When I launched it, everybody just FROZE, and it felt like time stood still. And all anybody could do was watch as the ball flew through the air.

213

And when the ball went through the net at the
other side of the court, you could hear a pin drop.

My shot was good for three points, which put the Funky Dunkers ahead by one. And when the final buzzer went off, my new teammates SWARMED me.

I finally got to see how it felt to be the HERO for once, and for the first time, I could see why everybody's always making a big deal about sports.

HOP HOP

In fact, I was thinking that this would make a good MOVIE. So I started working on getting signatures from my new teammates.

I gotta say, Mom was right about sports bringing people together. After the game, me and the guys went out for ice cream. And we were having so much fun that we decided to have SECONDS.

We were even talking about getting the team together and doing this all over again NEXT year. And even though that could be fun, I think sometimes you should just quit while you're ahead.

ACKNOWLEDGMENTS

Thanks to my wife, Julie, for being so supportive and encouraging, and thanks to my whole family for being in my corner all these years.

It takes a lot of people to make a book! Thanks to Charlie Kochman for your care and your expert help in making these books the best they can be. Thanks to everyone at Abrams, especially Michael Jacobs, Andrew Smith, Elisa Gonzalez, Hallie Patterson, Melanie Chang, Kim Lauber, Mary O'Mara, Alison Gervais, and Borana Greku. Thanks also to Steve Roman.

Thanks to the Wimpy Kid team: Shaelyn Germain-Dupre, Vanessa Jedrej, and Anna Cesary. Thanks to Deb Sundin, Kym Havens, and the whole team at An Unlikely Story.

Thanks to Rich Carr and Andrea Lucey for your outstanding support. Thanks to Paul Sennott for your expert advice. Thanks to Sylvie Rabineau and Keith Fleer for everything you do for me. Thanks to Roland Poindexter, Ralph Milero, Vanessa Morrison, and Michael Musgrave for bringing Greg Heffley's world to life in such a wonderful way.

Thanks also to Jess Brallier for your encouragement and friendship.

ABOUT THE AUTHOR

Jeff Kinney is a #1 *New York Times* bestselling author and a six-time Nickelodeon Kids' Choice Award winner for Favorite Book. Jeff has been named one of *Time* magazine's 100 Most Influential People in the World. He spent his childhood in the Washington, D.C., area and moved to New England, where he and his wife own a bookstore named An Unlikely Story.